GRUMPY DAD
SHOVELS SNOW

BY
TOM ROMITA

ART BY
NICK GUARRACINO

Grumpy Dad Shovels Snow
By Tom Romita
1st Edition, printed 11.17
Library of Congress Control Number:
2017917102

I love mornings!

Mornings are when I find out
all the fun things I am going to
do that day.

I love winter mornings most of all!

I love my woolly socks
and my puffy coat
and my fuzzy mittens

and I love running
and jumping in the snow
and making snowmen
and snow women
and snow angels
and snow sharks
and snow hippos
and ooh......!!!

DADA'S UP!!

"DADA! DADA!" I say.
"Can we go play in the snow?
Build a snow tower? Make giant
snow cupcakes? Ooohhh DADA!
Can you be a snow horsey?!"

"Coffee," my Dada says.

Sometimes I don't think Dada
loves mornings as much as I do.

Or snow.

"Molly, give Dad a minute,"
my Mama says. "He's not all awake yet."
"He looks awake," I say.

"Was that a minute?"

"No," my Dada says. I love my Dada,
but sometimes, he's grumpy.

"What's a minute?" I ask. I'm not
sure he heard me. "Dada? DADA!!"

"MOLLY. JANE. TERWILLIGER."

Sometimes when he's grumpy, my Dada calls me by all three of my names.

"What?" I ask.

"Please stop talking," he says grumpily. "For just a little while. OK?"

"OK," I say. "Can I talk to Mama?"

"Yes," he says.

"Mama?" I say.

"Yes, dear?"

"Why is Dada grumpy?"

"I'm not sure," she says and looks at Dada. "Tom, what's the matter?"

"It snowed," my Dada says. "Again."

"I have to shovel the walk. Again. I probably can't get to work. Again."

"YAAYYYYY!! SNOW DAYYYYY!!!" I scream.

"Dada?" I say
as he walks away.

"Doesn't he love snow?" I ask.
"I think he used to..." my Mama says.

"But it's April," she says.

Sometimes when my Dada is grumpy,
he says words that I get in trouble
for saying.

"MAMA!" I yell.
"Yes, Molly?"
"Can we go play in the snow?"
"Yes," my Mama says. "Just leave your Dada alone while he's shoveling."

"OK," I say.

"DADA!" I yell. "Hi!"
"Hi, Sweetheart," my Dada says.
"Please don't undo everything I just did."

"OK," I say. I don't know what 'undo' means. But COOL!! Dada made a huge pile of snow for me to play in!

"COWABUNGA!!!!"

Dada doesn't seem to think
it's as cool as I do.

"MOLLY! JANE! TERWILLIGER!"
Uh oh.

"Molly!" my Mama says.
"Come, let's play in the back yard."
"OK!" I say. "Mama, Dada is
still grumpy."

Mama and Nicky and I make a snowman and a snow woman and a snow dog and a snow robot that Mama calls a "Snobot." Mama says it is time for a break.

Hot chocolate is my favorite!

Uh oh, here comes Dada, and he still looks grumpy.

"Molly," he says. "Do you understand why I yelled at you?"

"Yes," I answer.

"Why?" he asks.

"Because you are grumpy," I say.

"Well, OK, yes," my Dada says. "But you understand that I have to shovel the driveway or we can't take the car anywhere, right?"

"Yes," I say.

"Like, say, in an emergency," he says. "Like the one we're having right now."

"Right now?" I ask, a little afraid.

"Oh, no. What??"

"Pizza. I need PIZZA!" my Dada says. "We have to go to Pizzapalooza now! It's an emergency!"

I don't think it's really an emergency.
I scream and yell because I am so happy!
Pizza is my favorite food, and Pizzapalooza
is my favorite place to eat pizza!

This is the BEST day EVER!

"Thanks Dada!" I say.
"You're welcome, my sweet little pepperoni pie," he says.

I'm happy I got to play in the snow and drink hot chocolate and eat pizza.

And I'm REALLY happy my Dada isn't grumpy anymore.

THE END.

MORE GRUMPY DAD ADVENTURES
COMING SOON!

56664804R00022

Made in the USA
Middletown, DE
15 December 2017